BALANCE BEAM BOSS

BY JAKE MADDOX

TEXT BY EMMA CARLSON BERNE
ILLUSTRATED BY KATIE WOOD

STONE ARCH BOOKS
a capstone imprint

Jake Maddox Girl Sports Stories are published by Stone Arch Books
a Capstone imprint
1710 Roe Crest Drive
North Mankato, Minnesota 56003
www.capstonepub.com

Library of Congress Cataloging-in-Publication Data
Names: Maddox, Jake, author. | Berne, Emma Carlson, author. | Wood, Katie, 1981– illustrator. | Maddox, Jake. Jake Maddox girl sports stories.
Title: Balance beam boss / by Jake Maddox ; text by Emma Carlson Berne ; illustrated by Katie Wood.
Description: North Mankato, Minnesota : an imprint of Stone Arch Books, [2019] | Series: Jake Maddox. Jake Maddox girls sports stories | Summary: Twelve-year-old Sofia Martinez is the best gymnast at Riverside Gymnastics Center, but when a fall from the balance beam, usually her best event, results in a concussion, she finds herself afraid of the beam, and equally afraid to tell anyone about her fear of falling—Sofia needs help before her trauma drives her away from gymnastics forever.
Identifiers: LCCN 2019000272| ISBN 9781496583253 (hardcover) | ISBN 9781496584519 (pbk.) | ISBN 9781496583277 (ebook pdf)
Subjects: LCSH: Gymnastics—Juvenile fiction. | Balance beam—Juvenile fiction. | Brain—Concussion—Juvenile fiction. | Self-confidence—Juvenile fiction. | Anxiety—Juvenile fiction. | CYAC: Gymnastics—Fiction. | Brain—Concussion—Fiction. | Self-confidence—Fiction. | Anxiety—Fiction. | Hispanic Americans—Fiction.
Classification: LCC PZ7.M25643 Bai 2019 | DDC 813.6 [Fic]—dc23
LC record available at https://lccn.loc.gov/2019000272

Designer: Tracy McCabe
Production Specialist: Katy LaVigne
Design Elements: Shutterstock

Printed and bound in the USA.
PA70

Table of Contents

CHAPTER 1

Gymnastics Love

Riverside Gymnastics Center always smelled of rubber and sweat and burnt sugar from the doughnut factory next door. But to twelve-year-old Sofia Martinez, it was the best smell on Earth.

No matter how late she'd been at the gym the night before, her heart always surged as she entered the vast space filled with beams and bars and ropes and mats. Riverside was her gym, but really, she often thought, it was her home.

"Sofia, wait!" called Rana, Sofia's best friend, as she climbed out of her mother's car and raced up to Sofia. "You think Coach is going to make us do push-ups today?"

Sofia held the heavy door open for her friend, who wore a purple hijab with her leotard today. Rana had chosen to start wearing a hijab when she turned twelve last month, and now she had a whole collection in all different colors.

"Ugh, hopefully not," Sofia replied. "Tia made tamales last night. I had like ten."

Sofia was living with her aunt, or *tia,* this year while her parents were with Doctors without Borders in Yemen. Home felt a little weird without Mom and Dad there, but they'd be back by Christmas—just six months away. And in the meantime, Tia Elizabeth was super nice and a great cook.

"Girls! Get going on warm-ups, then Sofia, I want to see you on the beam!" Coach Jackson shouted as Sofia and Rana entered the gym. The other members of the Riverside team were already stretching and running sprints.

Sofia and Rana dropped their bags and hurried to one of the mats to stretch. The eight Riverside gymnasts did their prances, pointing their toes with each step around the edge of the floor mat. Then they went through their planks, crunches, and side planks, designed to build core strength.

When her warm-up was finished, Sofia headed over to the balance beam. It was her strongest exercise. She liked the vault and the uneven bars fine, and floor was always fun, but the beam was where she felt the most at home.

Coach Jackson joined her. "Remember, our next meet is with Forest Hills," the coach said. "Their beam is particularly strong. We took first in uneven bars and beam last year. I want us to have just as strong a showing this year."

Sofia nodded. She'd win. She always did. One wall of her bedroom at home was solid blue with the fluttering satin of all her first-place ribbons.

A couple of other girls lined up to watch as Coach started Sofia's competition music—the *William Tell* Overture, which she loved.

"Now watch, girls!" Coach Jackson called. "I want you to see how Sofia focuses on the *setup* here. A lot of times we tend to focus on the flip itself. But the setup is just as important for a flip, because there is no time to correct in the air."

Sofia took a deep breath and swung onto the beam. The smooth, slightly nubby leather was familiar under her hands. She could feel her core muscles tighten. Her arms and legs balanced. The world looked right from up here. The beam was where she belonged.

She leapt to her feet, feeling her feet gripping the beam exactly right. Her heels were in the middle, toes to either side, like she was a gecko climbing up a wall. Her feet were sticky pads. They'd never let go of the beam.

The horns in Sofia's competition music sounded, and she brought her arms up in opening position. She made sure to keep her chin high, chest out, lower back straight, and legs perfectly poised.

As the music continued, Sofia pranced forward. Then she bent forward and lowered her hands to grip the beam.

Taking a deep breath, Sofia swung her pelvis and legs backward into a smooth back walkover. Then another, and another, her body whipping over her head, until she was back where she started.

"Nice!" Coach Jackson called.

The horns were picking up speed now. This was Sofia's favorite part: the layout step-out. It was basically a no-hands flip—a dramatic, difficult showstopper.

Sofia positioned herself, arms up, gaze straight ahead. She took a deep breath, then she tensed, feeling the power in her muscles. In a single movement, she launched herself off the beam and into the air.

Sofia's legs whipped up over her head, the momentum carrying her back down to the beam. Seconds later, her feet smacked onto the beam.

One more layout step-out, Sofia thought.

She prepared to launch herself off the beam, just as a loud *boom!* rang through the gym. Sofia startled. Her foot slipped slightly from its usual spot, pushing off an inch to the right. Her body lurched to regain control.

Go! she thought in a panic. *Just go!*

Sofia launched herself into the flip. Immediately, she knew it had been a mistake. If you started wrong, you could not correct in midair.

But the flip was happening. She was already in the air, upside down. Her momentum was carrying her up and over, but everything was in the wrong place. She couldn't sense where her body—or the beam—was in space.

Instead, she felt the fall.

CHAPTER 2

BEAM BRUISING

Sofia's body slammed into the beam, headfirst. Her spine rattled, and her head exploded in a burst of pain. She slipped, scrambling for the beam, but couldn't grab on. A second later, she hit the mats.

Through the ringing in her ears, Sofia heard her teammates gasp and Rana shout, "Sofia!"

A moment later, Coach Jackson leaned over her, touching her face. "Don't move," the coach said.

Sofia couldn't have moved if she'd wanted to. Coach Jackson ran her hands down Sofia's arms and legs.

"OK, turn your head back and forth," she said. "Now move your arms and legs."

Sofia groaned at the pain in her head and back. She tried to breathe deeply as Coach and Rana helped her sit up, but then nausea overwhelmed her. Leaning over, she threw up right on the mat.

"I'm so sorry," Sofia whispered, tears filling her eyes. "It was my fault. My foot was in the wrong spot."

"Yeah, I saw that," Coach said. "You know you can't execute a move like that if you don't start correctly. I've taught you that for years." She leaned over. "Honey, your pupils are different sizes. I think you might have a concussion."

Sofia closed her eyes against the blinding headache. "What was that sound?" she managed to ask. "That boom?"

"Just the door," Rana said gently. "The wind slammed it closed."

Sofia groaned. "It threw me off," she said.

She wished she could hide. Coach always made it clear that gymnasts only had themselves to blame if they went into a move without a perfect setup. Sofia had tried ever since she was six not to make a mistake like that. And now she had.

* * *

Dr. Berman withdrew the auriscope from Sofia's ear. "No skull fracture," she said. She gently moved Sofia's head back and forth. "And you say you vomited? Can you count backward from twenty by fours?"

"Twenty, sixteen, twelve, eight, four, zero . . . ," Sofia counted slowly.

She wanted to stop shaking but couldn't. Her head hurt so badly. She glanced at Tia, who was sitting very straight and stiff in the other chair. Tia had rushed to the gym as soon as Coach Jackson had called. She'd insisted that they drive straight to Dr. Berman's office.

Dr. Berman started typing on her laptop. "Well, with your pupils different sizes, the direct head hit, and the vomiting, I'd say you gave yourself a pretty good concussion, Sofia," she said.

Sofia started crying. She'd never had a concussion before. Sure, she'd had plenty of injuries—bruises, sprained fingers, shin splints. That came with being a gymnast. But she'd never had a head injury.

“When can I go back to the gym?” she asked. “I can’t take too much time off. I have meets to prepare for. My coach is counting on me!”

“You need a few weeks off,” Dr. Berman said. “Don’t go near the gym. We’ll do a follow-up visit, and once I clear you, you can start back. But I want you resting in the meantime. Got it?” Dr. Berman paused with her hand on the exam room doorknob.

Sofia nodded, looking at her lap. She didn’t want to rest. She wanted to travel back in time, before today ever happened.

CHAPTER 3

A Nightmare Secret

"I brought you gummy bears!" Rana's voice called from the front of the apartment.

Sofia quickly hopped down from her bed and started stretching on the floor. A moment later, Rana appeared in the doorway. Tia stood behind her, wearing her scrubs and a smile.

"I have to go in—the hospital just called," Tia said. "Don't overdo it with the exercises!"

"I won't," Sofia promised.

She pressed her legs into splits on the floor. It was amazing how much stiffer she'd gotten during just two weeks away from the gym. She focused on relaxing her hamstrings while keeping her leg muscles loose.

"Your splits are already better than mine, and I didn't even try to bust a hole in the beam with my skull," Rana said. She plopped down on Sofia's bed and tossed her a packet of gummy bears.

Sofia focused on the candy. "Mmm, thanks," she said. She ripped open the bag and bit the head off a red bear. "You're the best to come over every day like this."

A concussion and forced rest hadn't exactly felt like a vacation. The pain in Sofia's head had faded, but every time she thought about going back to the gym, she felt a sinking feeling in the pit of her stomach.

It was weird. She'd never felt that way after any of her other spills. After those injuries, all she could think about was getting back onto the equipment. She'd shown up every day to stretch with the team. Now she felt like she wanted to hide.

"I bet you can't wait to get back to the gym and see everyone else," Rana said.

Sofia pressed her face to her knee so she wouldn't have to look at her friend. Suddenly the image of the beam flying up to meet her, then the impact, slammed into her brain. It was as if it were happening all over again.

Sofia inhaled sharply. *What is wrong with me?* she thought. Every time someone brought up her accident—or going back to the gym—this happened. It was like she was reliving her injury all over again.

"So when are you coming back?" Rana asked. "I hate being there without you."

Sofia cleared her throat. "Dr. Berman cleared me this morning," she finally said.

"Oh, awesome!" Rana bounced up on the bed. "Have you told Coach?"

Sofia pretended to be fascinated with her carpet. "Yeah," she said. "I mean, no. I haven't told Coach."

Silence fell in the room. Sofia finally looked up at Rana. Her friend was giving her a strange look.

"What's going on?" Rana asked. "You're acting weird."

Sofia pressed her face back to her knee. She had to get away from Rana's gaze.

"I'm fine," she said. "Just quit asking me so many questions!"

The last words came out as a shout. Sofia glanced up. Rana's face grew blotchy, the way it always did when she was fighting back tears.

Shame welled up in Sofia. Not only was she letting down the team, now she was snapping at her best friend.

"OK, jeez," Rana muttered, climbing off the bed and heading for the door. "Forget I asked. Mom's getting my new leotard today. I'd better go home and try it on."

"Send me a picture!" Sofia called after her friend.

Once she was alone, Sofia curled up on the bed. She pulled her comforter up over her shoulders. She didn't want anyone—especially Rana—to know how much time she'd spent in this position the past couple of weeks.

Eventually Sofia drifted off to sleep. Almost immediately, the nightmare started again. She was back in the gym, on the beam. She could feel every detail—the grippy leather, the hard beam, her heart beating so loudly it seemed to fill the entire gym.

"Go!" Coach Jackson shouted, but her voice was distorted.

As if she were a puppet, Sofia felt herself whirling on the beam. She could sense what was coming, but she couldn't stop her body.

"Stop! Stop!" Sofia cried out to her dream self. But she couldn't. It was like Coach Jackson was controlling her somehow.

Then it came—the *boom!*

Sofia's foot slipped, and she was whirling one last time. She knew what was coming—she always did. Her head was going to hit the beam.

Sofia started awake, gripping her pillow, sweat covering her body. She flung the covers off to get some air and tried to slow her breath.

She hadn't told anyone—not Rana, not her coach, not Tia—about the nightmare that had been coming every night since the accident. And no matter what she did, Sofia couldn't seem to get her fall out of her head.

CHAPTER 4

Back on the Beam

"Sofia, glad you're back," Coach Jackson said a few days later. She glanced up from her clipboard as the other gymnasts crowded around.

Sofia stood next to Rana, who was wearing her new leotard, which was loose, with long arms and legs, and a matching hijab.

"You look so pretty," Sofia whispered to her. Rana rolled her eyes. Sofia could tell she hated having to wear it. But her parents wouldn't let her compete in a regular one.

"All recovered?" the coach asked briskly. She glanced at Sofia's doctor's note.

"Yep!" Sofia said, forcing a perkiness she didn't feel. "Dr. Berman says I'm all clear."

Physically, at least, Sofia thought to herself. She wasn't so sure about mentally. The nightmares had been particularly bad last evening. This morning at breakfast, Tia had asked why she looked so pale.

I can't avoid the gym forever, Sofia told herself. *Once I get back on the beam, I'll be fine. I have to be strong.*

"Well, good. We've got the meet with Forest Hills on Saturday," her coach reminded her. "I need you in top form."

Sofia's stomach dropped to her feet. She had forgotten all about the Forest Hills meet—probably because it was no big deal. Or at least, it used to be no big deal.

She nodded and tried to avoid looking at the beam in the corner of the gym. It was like a monster waiting to swallow her. Nausea rose up in her belly. She imagined her head hitting the wood.

I'm fine. I'm fine. I'm fine, Sofia said over and over, trying to convince herself.

"Once you're warmed up, get on the uneven bars and let's see a little workout, OK?" Coach said. Without waiting for an answer, she strode off to where some of the younger girls were trying handstands.

Sofia picked a spot on the mat and got to work. She tried to ignore the stiffness in her shoulders and hamstrings when she stretched.

I just need a little workout to loosen me up, she told herself. She went through the warm-up, then jogged toward the uneven bars.

Coach Jackson looked up. "Go ahead!" she called.

Sofia nodded and took a deep breath. The bars looked so high. They'd never looked that way before.

Stop being weird, Sofia scolded herself. She dipped her hands in the chalk near the bars. Then she took her spot in front of the lower bar and jumped up to grab it.

But the moment Sofia's hands hit the bar, something felt wrong. She wobbled, hoisting herself up, her arms shaking with the effort.

What if I fall? Sofia thought in a sudden panic.

It was a thought she'd never had before—not once in six years of training. She let go of the bar and let herself fall back to the mat.

"What's wrong, Sofia?" Coach called. "Head feeling OK? You're not dizzy, are you?"

"I'm OK!" Sofia called back.

She hoped the anxiety in her voice wasn't obvious. She remembered what Coach Jackson had said to one of the other gymnasts when she'd been scared to try a front-handspring entry on the vault: "There's no room for fear. You have the skills. Now you have to let your body take over. If you're afraid, you're not cut out for gymnastics."

Sofia swallowed back the sour bile that had risen in her throat at the memory.

"Well, listen, get on the beam, OK?" Coach called. "Rana's done."

Sofia nodded, not trusting her voice. She turned to face the beam, standing alone on the blue mat. It had always been her friend. But now her hands shook just looking at it.

I can't do it. I can't. I can't, Sofia thought in a sudden panic.

For a moment it was as if her body really *couldn't* move. But then she was hoisting herself onto the beam. She was up, balancing.

"Let's go through the routine from before you fell!" Coach Jackson called. "This is going to be your opening event at the Forest Hills meet. Ready?"

Sofia's chest was so tight, her heart seemed to be trying to hammer its way out of the tight bands around her ribs. Her breath was coming in little choking gasps as she stared down at the four-inch-wide beam in front of her feet.

She couldn't do this. But she couldn't get Coach Jackson's words out of her head: "If you're afraid, you're not cut out for gymnastics."

CHAPTER 5

"Get Out of Your Head!"

"Go, Sofia!"

Rana's voice cut through the fog in Sofia's head. She looked over at her friend, her purple hijab framing her face. She held on to the encouragement in Rana's eyes and forced her body to move backward into the first backflip.

But in an instant, she could tell she was going to fall. There was nothing she could do.

Sofia felt her foot slide down off the beam. A moment later, she smacked down, banging her pelvis on the beam.

She found herself straddling the beam, her hips aching and one fingernail bleeding where she'd ripped it trying to grab on.

Sofia leaned over, trying to catch her breath. A moment later, Coach Jackson's face swam into view, her brow creased.

"Up you go!" she said, thrusting her hand out.

Sofia took it shakily, climbing to her feet. *There's no room for fear,* she told herself. *If you're afraid, you're not cut out for gymnastics.*

"All right, back on the stick!" the coach said, pulling her hand away long before Sofia was ready to let go. "Come on! Get out of your head!"

It was something Coach said a lot when the girls were psyching themselves out over a hard move. It meant not overthinking things, letting your muscle memory take over.

Sofia was an expert at just shutting out the world and turning off her mind. The trouble was, now it felt like the spigot was broken. She couldn't seem to find that "off" handle in her mind. She couldn't stop thinking.

"You're OK, Sofia!" Rana called. A few other gymnasts chimed in.

Sofia cringed. She had an audience now. There was no choice. She braced herself on the beam, all her muscles tense.

I can't, I can't do it, I can't, I'm going to fall, I can't, her mind chanted. The beam looked about an inch wide. The floor on either side dropped away as if she were fifty feet up instead of four.

"I-I'm going to throw up," Sofia choked out. "I think I ate something bad." She scrambled off the beam, stumbling awkwardly to the mat.

As she ran for the locker room, she saw her teammates' shocked faces. But worse than that, she caught a glimpse of Coach Jackson, her lips pressed together, shaking her head.

* * *

That night, the nightmare came again. "*Go!*" Coach Jackson shouted.

Like always, Sofia's body whirled off the beam. The fear filled her. She clawed at the air as she pinwheeled, her head aiming for the beam.

Sofia woke up gasping, her cheeks wet with tears. She lay back in bed, her heart hammering, and stared up at the ceiling above.

What is happening to me? she thought desperately.

She'd broken fingers in a floor routine. She'd sprained her ankle at least three times on vault *and* on the uneven bars dismount. She'd barely thought about those injuries, except to be annoyed at how long she was out of training.

But now she couldn't stop reliving that awful moment when everything went so out of control. All she could think about was falling, knowing the worst was about to happen.

Sofia threw back the covers, suddenly coated in sweat. The Forest Hills meet was the day after tomorrow. One thought kept running through her mind: *How am I going to win when I can't even get on the beam?*

CHAPTER 6

GO TIME

Sofia couldn't stop shaking. It was the day of the Forest Hills meet, and she was standing next to Rana and the rest of her team.

"What's wrong?" Rana asked. She touched Sofia's hand. "Your hands are all clammy. Are you still not feeling well?"

Sofia shook her head. It was all she could manage. Her throat seemed to have closed up. She opened her mouth to say something, to tell Rana how terrified she was, but before she could, the loudspeaker crackled to life.

"All competitors please proceed to the warm-up stations," the announcer's voice said. "Coaches to the judging table."

The Riverside gymnasts trotted to the mats. Sofia's hands were shaking so hard, she was sure someone would notice. But the others weren't paying attention, and Rana had been called up to the judges' table. She had to explain her hijab and leotard, like she needed to at practically every meet.

"Rana's on the uneven bars first," Coach Jackson said, bustling up to the group. "Get over there, Riverside, let's support her."

"Coach . . . ," Sofia said, but Coach Jackson had that focused look in her eyes she always got at a meet.

"Sofia, you're on beam next, OK?" the coach said. With that, she marched toward the bars, where Rana was chalking her hands.

Everyone gathered on the bleachers. Rana took a deep breath. She leapt up to the lower bar, smoothly rotating into her first handstand. Her body was as straight as an arrow balanced on top of the bar.

She swung down, then back up, rotating her grip. She used her momentum to fly to the upper bar, the wood thunking into her palms.

Rana flipped around the bar once, flew back to the lower bar for a rotation, then flew back to the upper. She did a perfect handstand on the upper, followed by another rotation, flipping her grip.

She flew to the lower bar next and rose into a standing position for one brief second, then reached for the upper bar in a straddle-back release. She whirled around and around the upper bar and flew to the lower, completely airborne for a moment.

It was time for the dismount. Rana swung once more around the bar, then released and flew through the air, twisting through one and a half somersaults. Sofia held her breath, and Rana's feet hit the mat. She made just one tiny hop back—she stuck the landing.

The Riverside gymnasts cheered as Rana flung her arms into the air. Then she trotted off the mat. Sofia jumped off the bleachers and hugged her friend.

Sweat ran down Rana's face. "How was it?" she asked, beaming.

"How do you think?" Sofia said. "Perfect." She grinned. For a few blissful minutes, she had forgotten everything as she watched her best friend compete.

Then Coach's voice brought her back to reality: "Sofia, beam!"

CHAPTER 7

BEAM DISASTER

The fear and dread Sofia had been carrying for days slammed into her. She had to do the beam. Except she couldn't. She knew she couldn't.

Somehow Sofia found herself on the mat. The beam loomed in front of her. Her breath came in gasps. She couldn't feel her hands.

"Athlete, please begin," the head judge spoke into the microphone. A mechanical *beep* sounded through the gym, signaling the start of judging.

Sofia felt like she was trapped in her nightmare. She was going to fall. She could sense it. She stared at the beam, and all she could see was her head hitting it.

Move! Sofia screamed inside herself. *You can't let your team down. You can't let Coach Jackson down. Move! Everyone is counting on you.*

"Go, Sofia!" someone shouted behind her.

The music started, and Sofia forced herself to walk forward.

Get on the beam, she ordered herself. *Get on.*

She was supposed to run forward and jump up to mount the beam. But her wooden legs wouldn't do that. There was no way.

Sofia walked forward like a robot. Panicky, she tried to scramble up onto the beam. It was a move she hadn't used since she was a five-year-old novice.

Sofia's ragged breathing seemed to echo in the gym. She fumbled with the beam, one leg up on it and the other foot still on the ground. She grunted, then fell to the mat with a thud.

"Sofia?" someone said quietly beside her.

Sofia looked up. Coach Jackson stood there. The coach slipped a strong hand under Sofia's arm and hoisted her to her feet.

"What's wrong?" she asked. "Are you sick?"

Sofia looked up at her coach's concerned face. She opened her mouth, then closed it.

Finally, she made the words come out—words she'd needed to say since her injury.

"I need help," she croaked.

Coach Jackson put her arm around Sofia's shoulders, shielding her from the shocked stares. "And you're going to get it," she said. "I'll make sure of that."

CHAPTER 8

Coach Can Help

Out in the hall, Coach Jackson motioned for Sofia to take a seat in a hard, plastic chair. Sofia obeyed, practically collapsing into it.

"Now," she said, "it was clear something was wrong out there. Something was wrong at practice too, but you said you were just sick. Was that true? Or is there something else going on?"

Sofia clenched her hands between her knees. Hot tears stung her eyes.

There was no way she could go back out there. There was no way she could face her teammates again. She had let herself—and everyone else—down. She had embarrassed the whole team.

Coach Jackson pulled up another chair so that their knees were almost touching. She leaned forward. "Sofia, talk to me."

Sofia's eyes darted from Coach Jackson to the door. If she moved fast, she might be able to make a break for it. Then the door opened. Rana walked in, holding a chocolate bar.

"I bought this from the vending machine," she said, handing it to Sofia. "I know we're not supposed to eat, Coach, but I figured this was a special situation."

Escape route blocked.

"Can I stay?" Rana asked.

Coach Jackson looked at Sofia, who nodded. Rana came to stand next to her, and Sofia groped for her hand.

"I know I've had injuries before," she started. "We all have. But this one . . . feels different. I don't know why. But ever since I fell I've been having nightmares. I feel like the beam is some kind of monster. I keep seeing the accident over and over again. And when I'm on the beam, I just feel so tense and scared. Everything in my body just feels *off*."

"Why didn't you say anything?" Coach Jackson asked. Her voice was full of distress.

Sofia hesitated. "I was afraid to," she said, looking down at her knees. "I didn't want to be weak. I didn't want to let you down. You always say there's no room for fear. That if we're afraid, we aren't cut out for gymnastics."

Coach was silent for a minute. "I do say that," she said. "It's something my coach used to say to me. I thought I was encouraging you girls to conquer your fears. But clearly that isn't the case." She squeezed Sofia's hands. "Listen, let me do a little thinking. We're going to figure this out, and we're going to do it together."

CHAPTER 9

HARD WORK, HARD RECOVERY

A few days later, Sofia shifted uneasily on a bench at the Riverside gym. Rana was there, sitting right beside her, along with the rest of her teammates. She hadn't seen any of them since the meet.

A moment later, Coach Jackson walked into the gym with an unfamiliar woman. She had a no-nonsense haircut and a lined face that looked like she spent a lot of time outdoors.

"Girls, this is Dr. Wigton," Coach said, motioning to the woman with her. "She's a sports counselor, and I've arranged for her to talk to us about trauma. More specifically, how trauma can affect us all during our sports careers."

Sofia's face flamed. Dr. Wigton was here because of *her*. She wanted to crawl under the bench and hide. But no one else seemed to make the connection. They all had their eyes fixed on Dr. Wigton as if they were really interested.

"Sports injuries and accidents do happen in gymnastics, as all of you know," Dr. Wigton said. "And sometimes we focus just on the physical recovery. But did you girls know that your brain might need recovery too?"

Sofia didn't say anything.

"A sports injury can be as traumatic as a car accident," Dr. Wigton went on. "Sometimes athletes even have mild symptoms of post-traumatic stress disorder—PTSD. It might be having nightmares about the injury, feeling anxious about coming back to the gym, even having panic attacks."

Rana squeezed Sofia's hand. Sofia's heart was beating loud. She cast a careful glance at the others. No one was staring at her like she was some kind of freak. In fact, no one was looking at her at all. They were all listening to Dr. Wigton as if she might be giving *them* answers too.

"These feelings are normal," Dr. Wigton said. "But a lot of times, athletes worry there's something wrong with them. There's not. But there are things you can do to help move past the trauma."

Sofia's eyes were locked firmly on Dr. Wigton's face. For the first time since her injury, she felt hopeful rather than terrified.

* * *

"So, your coach tells me you've had a hard time recovering from a bad fall on the beam," Dr. Wigton said an hour later. She, Sofia, and Coach Jackson were all in the coach's office.

Sofia nodded, her hands squeezed tightly between her knees. "A lot of the things you said out there—they happened to me," she admitted.

Dr. Wigton nodded. "Coach Jackson filled me in. If you'd like, I can give you a treatment plan to help you move past your injury."

Sofia nodded. There was nothing she wanted more.

"OK," Dr. Wigton said. "We'll start with baby steps. When the gym is quiet, and you're feeling calm, you and Coach Jackson will approach the beam. First, you'll just touch it, pat it. Then, you'll sit on it. That's it. The next time, you'll walk up and down the beam. Then, when you're ready, you'll do one back walkover. The next day, two, and the next—"

"Three," Sofia put in. "That doesn't sound too scary."

"Right!" Dr. Wigton said. "The trick is not to move on to the next part of the routine until you're comfortable with the previous part."

Sofia nodded again. That made sense to her.

"The very last thing you'll do is recreate the trauma," Dr. Wigton continued. "In your case, that's the noise that startled you. Repeating the event that caused the injury can help take away the power it has over you."

"OK," Sofia said. "Let's give it a try."

CHAPTER 10

Back to the Beam

"Back walkover!" Coach Jackson called two days later. She looked at the paper in her hand. "Your routine has you doing it three times, but do you want to start with once?"

Sofia nodded and flipped smoothly back into the back walkover. She was on day three of Dr. Wigton's plan. For the first time in weeks, she wasn't afraid.

"I think I can do it twice more," she said after she finished. Something about knowing she didn't *have* to do it made it easier to do.

Before her coach could protest, Sofia braced her hands against the beam and whipped her legs up again, then once more. It was the first time since her accident that being upside down had felt right.

"OK, that's it for today," Coach called.

Sofia slid off the beam. "It feels weird only doing one part of the routine," she said.

Coach smiled. "I know. But just think of it as doctor's orders."

The next day, Sofia and Coach were back at it. They practiced another part of her routine. The following day, they did it again.

"I want to try something new today," Coach said Friday, looking up at Sofia on the beam. "I called Dr. Wigton last night to update her on your progress, and she recommended that I slam the door during your flip."

A tiny bit of fear knifed through Sofia's stomach. She forced herself to take a deep breath. "OK," she said, nodding.

"Are you sure?" Coach Jackson asked. "We don't have to do it if you're not comfortable."

"No, I want to," Sofia said. She was starting to feel like her old self. She didn't want to give that up. "I want to do it all now. I don't want to leave anything to chance."

Coach Jackson nodded and took a step back. Sofia positioned herself at the end of the beam, and her coach started the music.

Sofia heard the horns signaling the start of her routine. Three back walkovers—one, then another, then another. Then the layout step-out. No hands.

Her body aligned itself. Sofia shut off her mind and let her body take over, the way Coach Jackson had taught her.

Then she did the next layout step-out and there it was—*boom!*—just as Sofia was in midair. It was muffled and dull, not the sharp, jarring noise she remembered. Maybe it had sounded like that all along and she'd imagined a much scarier sound?

Sofia's feet hit the beam—not perfect, but solid—and she let out a huge breath. She'd done it. The whole routine. And she hadn't fallen once.

Sofia turned and grinned. It hadn't been easy, and she wasn't all the way there, but she'd done it. She'd faced her trauma and found her way back to the beam.

Author Bio

Emma Carlson Berne has written numerous historical and biographical books for children and young adults, as well as young adult fiction. She lives in Cincinnati, Ohio, with her husband and two sons.

Illustrator Bio

Katie Wood fell in love with drawing when she was very small. Since graduating from Loughborough University School of Art and Design in 2004, she has been living her dream working as a freelance illustrator. From her studio in Leicester, England, she creates bright and lively illustrations for books and magazines all over the world.

GLOSSARY

auriscope (AWR-uh-skohp)—an instrument with a light used for examining the ear

bile (bahyl)—a thick, bitter yellow or greenish fluid produced by the liver to aid in digestion of fats in the small intestine

concussion (kuhn-KUHSH-uhn)—an injury to the brain caused by a hard hit on the head

distress (dih-STRES)—a great suffering of body or mind

execute (EK-si-kyoot)—to carry out or perform

hijab (he-JAHB)—a traditional scarf worn by Muslim women to cover the hair, neck, and sometimes the face

momentum (moh-MEN-tuhm)—the characteristic of a moving body that is caused by its mass and its motion

trauma (TRAW-muh)—a serious bodily injury caused by an accident or violent act, or an abnormal psychological or behavioral state resulting from severe mental or emotional stress or injury

vast (vahst)—very great in size or amount

Discussion Questions

1. Sofia is hesitant to talk about her fears with her best friend, her coach, and her aunt. How do you think her story would have been different if she'd been open about her fears from the start?

2. Sofia's fall is scary and traumatic for her. Talk about a time something scary or upsetting happened to you. What did you do to help yourself through the incident?

3. Coaches and teachers offer a support system for students and players. They can also sometimes push students or players too far or not far enough. Talk about a time that a coach or teacher supported you. Then talk about a time when you did not feel supported by a coach or teacher.

Writing Prompts

1. Rana is Sofia's best friend, but she also has her own story to tell. Choose a scene in this story and rewrite it from Rana's perspective. How does the scene change when Rana is telling the story?

2. Sofia loves gymnastics and pushes herself hard. Make a list of five activities you love to do. Do you push yourself to do better at these activities, like Sofia? Why or why not?

3. This book begins after Sofia's parents leave for their work trip. Give the book a different beginning: show us Sofia saying goodbye to her parents. What kinds of thoughts and emotions can you express through dialogue?

Gymnastics Glossary

BACK WALKOVER

a gymnastic move in which a person leans forward to perform a handstand, then arches backward to a similar handstand and moves the feet to the floor

BALANCE BEAM

a piece of gymnastic equipment that is a narrow, horizontal beam raised off the floor

CORE

the muscles that lie deep in the pelvis, abdomen, and rear end

LAYOUT STEP-OUT

a gymnastic jump in which a gymnast jumps with both feet, pushing the body upward, and flips in the air with legs together, landing first on one foot, then on the other

PELVIC MUSCLES

muscles that lie like a hammock across the pelvis and support the pelvic organs

PRANCES

high, springy steps

UNEVEN BARS

a pair of parallel bars set at different heights; part of women's gymnastic equipment

VAULT

a piece of gymnastic equipment similar to a table, which the gymnast uses as a springboard for flips and other maneuvers

THE FUN DOESN'T STOP HERE!

Discover more:

VIDEOS & CONTESTS
GAMES & PUZZLES
HEROES & VILLAINS
AUTHORS & ILLUSTRATORS

www.capstonekids.com